CARTOON NETWORK™

SCOOBY-DOO!™

AND THE

BOWLING
BOOGEYMAN

Look for these recent **Scooby-Doo Mysteries**.
Collect as many as you can!

SCOOBY-DOO!
AND THE
BOWLING BOOGEYMAN

Written by
James Gelsey

A
LITTLE APPLE
PAPERBACK

SCHOLASTIC INC.

New York   Toronto   London   Auckland   Sydney
Mexico City   New Delhi   Hong Kong   Buenos Aires

ISBN 0-439-42071-7

Designed by Carisa Swenson

12 11 10 9 8 7 6 5   4 5 6 7/0

Special thanks to Duendes del Sur for cover and interior illustrations.
Printed in the U.S.A.
First Scholastic printing, September 2002

For the real Scooby

Special thanks to Larry W.
and the gang at Bowler City.

Chapter 1

"There it is, gang!" Fred announced. "Drury Lanes, home of the Bowlfest." He steered the Mystery Machine into a large parking lot.

"The Bowlfest? I thought Drury Lanes was home of the Muffin Man," Shaggy said.

"What Muffin Man, Shaggy?" asked Daphne.

"You know, like, the children's song," Shaggy said. "Sing it with me, Scoob."

"'Rave rou reen ruh Ruffin Ran,'" sang Scooby.

"'The Muffin Man, the Muffin Man,'" Shaggy continued. "'Have you seen the Muffin Man . . .'"

"'Roo rives ron Rury Rane,'" Scooby sang.

"Speaking of muffins," Shaggy said, "I sure wouldn't mind a little chocolate chip muffin action about now. I'm hungry."

Fred turned off the ignition and turned around in his seat. "Shaggy, Drury Lanes is the name of the bowling alley," he said. "And tonight's the big Bowlfest, remember?"

"Hey, tonight's the big Bowlfest, Scooby!" Shaggy said. "Like, what's the big Bowlfest?"

"Climb out of the van, and we'll explain," Velma said. Everyone jumped out of the van. They stood looking up at the sign for the Drury Lanes Bowling Alley.

"Bowlfest is a charity bowling tournament," Daphne said. "We signed up for it months ago, remember?"

"And it's not our fault you never came with us to practice," Velma said.

Shaggy and Scooby just looked at each other and shrugged.

"What's the big deal, Velma?" asked Shaggy. "We're just, like, rolling a ball at some pins to knock them down. Why did we need to practice?"

"So you'd know what to do if you bowled a split, for instance," Fred said.

"A split? As in banana split?" Shaggy asked.

"Rum!" Scooby said, licking his lips.

"No, not a banana split," Velma said, laughing. "A seven-ten split. It's when the two corner pins are left standing. They're the hardest things to knock down. But if you do, you get a spare."

"A spare? Like, what would I do with an extra tire at a bowling alley?" Shaggy wondered.

"It's not a spare tire, Shaggy," Daphne said. "It's what they call it when you knock down all the pins in two tries. And if you knock them down in one try, you get a strike."

"Zoinks!" Shaggy said. "We'd better be careful not to get three of those, Scoob. Otherwise, we'll be out."

Fred, Daphne, and Velma rolled their eyes.

"It's not baseball, Shaggy," Fred said. "Strikes are good."

"I don't know about you, Scooby, but I never realized bowling was so confusing," Shaggy said. "Maybe we'd better just skip the Bowl-fest and go to this charity eating tournament down the street."

"What charity eating event down the street?" asked Daphne.

"Pizzafest!" Shaggy joked.

"Very funny, Shaggy," Velma said. "But we already promised to go bowling for charity. So forget about the pizza and let's go inside."

Shaggy and Scooby sighed and followed the others beneath a WELCOME TO BOWLFEST banner. Once inside, the sounds of bowling pins crashing filled their ears.

"Jinkies!" Velma said. "I forgot how loud bowling alleys can be."

As the gang walked over to the control desk, they heard a woman yelling behind them. "Where's the manager? I demand to see the manager!" she hollered.

A tall man in a blue-and-orange bowling shirt with the number 9 on the back rushed out from behind the control desk.

"What's the matter?" he asked the woman.

"If I had wanted food with my bowling ball, I would have gone to the snack bar," she said, holding up her hand.

The man studied the brown goo stuck to the woman's fingers.

"Not again!" he moaned. "I'm sorry, ma'am. It's just peanut butter. Someone's been stuffing peanut butter into some of the bowling balls.

Why don't you go wash up and enjoy your entire game for free."

The woman just stared at him without moving.

"Including your shoe rental."

The woman still did not move. "For you and all of your friends."

Still no movement.

"Tonight and the next time you visit Drury Lanes."

Finally, the woman nodded and marched off to the bathroom.

"I wonder why someone would put peanut butter in bowling ball finger holes," Daphne said.

"Maybe they don't want to have to stop bowling to have a snack," Shaggy said.

"Or maybe someone's trying to send a message to the bowling alley," Fred said.

"What kind of message?" asked Daphne.

"I have a hunch we'll find out soon enough," Velma said.

Chapter 2

The man in the blue-and-orange shirt carried the peanut-buttered bowling ball back to the control desk.

"Excuse me, we're here for the bowling tournament," Fred said.

"Sign in, and make sure to include your shoe sizes," the man said, sliding a piece of paper to Fred. Fred wrote down everyone's names. The man checked the names and then looked at the roster attached to a clipboard.

"Hey, you're on my team." He smiled. "Nine-Pin Hooper, at your service."

"Hi, Mr. Hooper, I'm Fred. And this is

Daphne, Velma, Shaggy, and Scooby-Doo," Fred said.

"Glad to have you on my team, kids," Nine-Pin said. "We're going to be starting in a little while, so if you want to go warm up, use lane nine. It's my lucky lane."

"Thanks, Mr. Hooper," Daphne said.

"Not so fast, kids," said a man in coveralls as he walked up to the counter. He set down a toolbox and held up a black belt from a motor. The belt had been torn into two long pieces.

"Bad news, boss. Nine's out of commission. The main belt's snapped and the ball booster is shot. I'll get to work on it, but I can't promise anything." The man walked toward the lanes and disappeared through a door.

Nine-Pin shook his head slowly. "Just my luck," he said. "First the peanut butter in the bowling balls. Now my lucky lane's busted. What else can go wrong with this event?"

"Would you like the list in alphabetical order?" another voice said. The gang turned and saw a man wearing a short-sleeved shirt and black pants. A tiny silver bowling ball pin glistened on his shirt. His black hair was slicked back, and he had a pencil-thin moustache perched over his upper lip. He held a brown bowling ball bag in his left hand.

"What do you want, Anndegs?" Nine-Pin asked.

"You to admit that my bowling alley is much nicer than this place," the man said. "After all, Bowlers' Paradise offers thirty-six lanes of peanut-butter-free bowling."

"If your bowling alley is so wonderful, why is everyone still coming here?" asked Nine-Pin.

"I signed up to bowl in the tournament to find out," the man said.

As Nine-Pin looked over the tournament roster, the man noticed the gang looking at him.

"Yes, yes, you do recognize me," the man said. "I'm Hamilton Anndegs, famous professional bowler. You probably know me as "'Ten Hamilton,'" because I bowl strikes all the time. And I'll bet you can guess why they call him Nine-Pin, can't you?" Hamilton Anndegs gave Nine-Pin a mean little grin.

"Now that he's retired, he runs a bowling

alley across town," Nine-Pin said. "And since he's no longer on the bowling tour, you can call him what we all do. Ham."

"Ham Anndegs?" Shaggy said. He and Scooby began to giggle.

"You're just jealous that I have one of these and you don't," Hamilton Anndegs said, pointing to his pin. "It's the Ten-K Striker Pin for making more than ten thousand lifetime strikes," he explained to the kids. Then he turned back to Nine-Pin. "It seems

that just about everyone on the tour earned one — except you."

"You're just jealous because I beat you in your last tournament," Nine-Pin replied.

Hamilton Anndegs just laughed. "See you on the lanes, Hooper," he said. "Unless you're too scared." He picked up his brown bowling ball bag and walked away.

"What was that all about, Nine-Pin?" asked Fred.

"If I tell you kids, you have to promise not to tell a soul," Nine-Pin said.

"We promise," Daphne said. "Right, fellas?"

Shaggy and Scooby nodded.

"The last time we bowled together professionally, I caught Hamilton cheating," Nine-Pin said. "When the bowling association found out, they banned him from the tour. You might say his retirement was not entirely voluntary."

"So he's mad at you because he got caught cheating?" Velma asked.

Nine-Pin nodded.

"What do you say we warm up?" Fred said.

"You can use lane eighteen on the far end," Nine-Pin said as he handed the gang their bowling shoes. "Maybe it'll be twice as lucky as lane nine."

"Thanks, Nine-Pin," Daphne said. "We'll see you over there. Come on, everyone. Let's go bowling!"

Chapter 3

Fred, Daphne, Velma, Shaggy, and Scooby grabbed their bowling shoes and headed over to lane eighteen at the far end of the bowling alley. They passed a tall stand holding a large silver bowling pin trophy.

"Wow, that is beautiful," Daphne gasped.

"Thank you," said a woman next to them. She was also admiring it.

"You're welcome," Daphne said. "Are you the artist who designed the trophy?"

"I'm not an artist, and I didn't exactly design it," the woman said. "I'm Barbara Carbonara, president of Bowl-Rite, Inc. We make all the bowling equipment you see here in the alley. I paid for the trophy."

"Barbara Carbonara?" Shaggy whispered to Scooby. "Is it me, or does everyone's name around here remind you of food?"

"Reah, rood," Scooby agreed.

"Ah, Barbara," Nine-Pin said as he walked over. "The trophy looks incredible."

"Too bad no one's going to see it," Barbara said.

"What do you mean?" asked Fred. "Everyone in the tournament's going to see it."

"She means that there aren't enough people in the tournament," Nine-Pin explained. "And not enough press here to cover it."

"Last year, this event was the biggest thing in town," Barbara said. "But ever since people started finding peanut butter in their bowling balls, they've been canceling left and right. Even the TV stations are staying away."

"Listen, Barbara, I've been making Wylie work double shifts to make sure no one messes with the tournament," Nine-Pin said. "Maybe people just aren't interested in bowling anymore."

"And maybe I just don't feel like giving this very expensive trophy to the handful of average bowlers you've attracted to this event," Barbara countered. "I mean, if I'm one of the only people here with a Ten-K Striker Pin, then maybe we should just call the whole thing off!"

"Jeepers, Ms. Carbonara," Daphne said. "I

thought we were doing this for charity. I mean, isn't that what it's all about?"

"It's about publicity and selling bowling shoes, honey," Barbara Carbonara said. "And unless there's some action here tonight, I'm taking my business and sponsorships over to Bowlers' Paradise." The president of Bowl-Rite, Inc., marched off.

"Jinkies, she wasn't very nice," Velma said.

"She isn't," agreed Nine-Pin, "but she's got a point. I hope something exciting happens tonight, otherwise I'm afraid we'll be in trouble that's a lot more serious than peanut butter." Nine-Pin sighed and returned to the control desk.

"Shaggy, you and Scooby get some bowling balls," Fred said. "We'll take your shoes and meet you over at the lane."

"Right-o, Fred-o," Shaggy said. "Come on, Scooby."

Shaggy and Scooby walked over to the bowling ball rack.

"Now, let's see," Shaggy said. "What's it going to be? Black, blue, red, or one of those swirly-colored ones?"

"Ri runno." Scooby shrugged. "Row rabout rue?"

"Blue it is," Shaggy said. He reached over and started to put his fingers into the holes. Then he quickly pulled them out and lowered his face to the bowling ball.

"Better safe than sorry," he said, giving each hole a big sniff. "Nope, no peanut butter here." Then he put his fingers into the holes and lifted the bowling ball off the rack. "This one feels — WHOOOA!" The ball plummeted to the floor, yanking Shaggy's arm with it. "A little too heavy. Give me a paw, Scoob."

Scooby helped Shaggy pick up the bowling ball and return it to the rack.

19

"How about one of these with the gold stars on it?" Shaggy said.

This time, Scooby checked it out before Shaggy picked it up off the rack.

"Nice and light," Shaggy said. He put his fingers into the ball and pretended to bowl. Just as he raised his arm up behind him, the ball dropped from his fingers.

"Rouch!" Scooby cried, jumping up into the air. He grabbed the tip of his tail and blew on it.

"Sorry, pal," Shaggy said. "I guess the finger holes are a little too big. Your tail okay?"

"Reah," Scooby said.

"Man, I never knew it was so hard to find the right bowling ball," Shaggy said.

"Psst!" someone whispered.

Shaggy and Scooby looked around.

"PSST! Over here!" the voice said. It came from a dark doorway next to the bowling ball rack. "I've got just what you're looking for."

"A pizza?" asked Shaggy.

"The perfect bowling ball," the voice answered.

Chapter 4

Shaggy and Scooby slowly stepped back.
"On the count of three, we run," Shaggy whispered. "One . . . two . . ."

"Wait!" the voice whispered as a man stepped out of the shadows.

"AHH!" Shaggy cried.

It was the man in the coveralls they had seen earlier at the control desk.

"It's just me, Wylie Smithens," he said.

Shaggy and Scooby breathed a sigh of relief.

"Man, for a second there we thought you

were some kind of bowling monster or something," Shaggy said.

"I'm the bowling alley's head mechanic," Wylie said. "And I've got something to show you. Follow me."

Wylie turned and disappeared into the darkness. Shaggy and Scooby peered through the doorway, but didn't follow him. Wylie flicked on a dim lightbulb, illuminating a workshop.

"Come inside, and close the door behind you," Wylie instructed.

Shaggy and Scooby stepped inside.

"Here it is," Wylie said, lifting a brown bowling ball bag onto the workbench. He reached inside and took out a glistening black bowling ball. Tiny stars on the ball's surface glowed in the dim light.

"Nice bowling ball," Shaggy said. "But I don't think either of us is good enough to use something that nice. But thanks for thinking of us. We have to go now. Bye."

"Wait!" Wylie shouted. Shaggy and Scooby froze. "This is no ordinary bowling ball. This is my secret invention. I call it the Robowler."

"Robowler?" asked Scooby.

"Short for Robotic Bowling Ball," Wylie said. "When I was younger, I was a professional bowler. I was one of the first people to get one of these." He showed Shaggy and Scooby a tiny silver bowling pin stuck to his collar. "Ever since I stopped bowling, I've been working on an invention to make anyone a perfect bowler. And with all the double shifts I've been doing lately, I'm very close to finishing."

"It looks like a regular bowling ball to me," Shaggy said.

"It's not. It's a special bowling ball that you can program to knock down any pins you want," Wylie said. "It's got a gyroscopic maneuvering device inside that controls the ball's speed and angle of momentum. You want strikes all the time, you can get them. You want to knock down a seven-ten split, no problem. You want your friend to always get the gutter, you can do that, too. It'll revolutionize bowling everywhere."

"So, like, why are you showing it to us?" asked Shaggy.

"So you can use it in the tournament," Wylie said. "You'll outscore Nine-Pin and that snobby Ham Anndegs and show them all how anyone can beat a professional. Then they'll be begging to give me money to fund a full-scale Robowler factory."

"Thanks for thinking of us, man," Shaggy said. "But that would be, like, cheating. Catch you later."

Before Wylie could say anything else, Shaggy and Scooby bolted out the door. They saw Fred, Daphne, and Velma already warming up on lane eighteen.

"Where have you two been?" asked Velma.

"We were looking for bowling balls when the strangest thing happened," Shaggy said. He told them about their encounter with Wylie Smithens.

"Forget about that and put on your bowling shoes," Daphne said. "You've only got time for one warm-up ball."

Shaggy sat down and took off his shoes. He grabbed the red-and-white-striped bowling shoes and laced them up.

"Hey, these are groovy," he said, admiring them. "Look at me, I'm a soft-shoe dancer!" He stood up and started to do a little dance.

"Careful, Shaggy, the soles are pretty slippery," Fred warned.

"Not to worry, Fred, I've got excellent bala-a-a-a-a-aance," Shaggy said as he crashed to the floor.

"Ree-hee-hee-hee-hee," giggled Scooby.

"Knock it off, you two, the tournament's about to begin!" Daphne said.

Chapter 5

"Ladies and gentlemen, welcome to Drury Lanes' annual Bowlfest!" Nine-Pin announced over the PA system. "We'd like to thank our sponsor, Bowl-Rite, Inc., makers of bowling balls, shoes, and all the things you need to bring out the best bowler in you. If you want to bowl right, remember Bowl-Rite!"

A smattering of applause rose from the handful of lanes being used for the tournament.

"Remember the rules, bowlers," Nine-Pin

announced. "Highest score for one complete game wins. Ties will be broken by a single frame bowl-off. Two gutter balls and you're out. Any questions?"

For the first time all night, the bowling alley was completely silent.

"Then let's get bowling!" Nine-Pin called.

The alley roared back to life as bowling balls began rumbling down the lanes.

"Here we go, everyone," Fred said. "And remember, two gutter balls and you're out. So be extra-careful, Shaggy."

"Like, no problem, Fred," Shaggy said. He picked up a bowling ball and prepared to bowl. Just as he swung his arm back, a howling sound filled the bowling alley. Everyone froze.

"Zoinks! What was that?" Shaggy cried.

Another howl echoed through the bowling alley as someone shouted, "Look!"

Something crawled out from behind the bowling pins on lane nine. The creature had giant glow-in-the-dark eyes that glared at the

crowd. The monster raised one of its long hairy arms and waved its fierce-looking claws in the air.

"AAAARRRRRRRRRRRR!" it roared.

"What is it?" asked Daphne.

"Whatever it is, it's holding a brown bowling ball bag in its other hand," Velma said.

"Never mind that," Shaggy said. "It's coming toward us!"

"Rikes!" Scooby cried, jumping into Shaggy's arms. Shaggy lost his balance and his slippery bowling shoes shot out from un-

der him. He and Scooby landed on the floor with a thud.

The monster ran partway down the lane and then slid the rest of the way to the front. He turned to the bowlers in lanes ten and eight and made a "boooooogey" sound at them by shaking his head and letting his cheeks flap around. The bowlers jumped back.

The monster opened its bowling bag and took out a shiny black ball and rolled it down the lane. The ball crashed into the pins, knocking them all down.

Then everyone ducked down as the monster ran over to the trophy stand. It reached up and grabbed the giant silver bowling pin, holding it high over its head.

"AAAAH-OOOOOOOOOOOOO!"

The creature ran back to lane nine, slid all the way to the end, and disappeared behind the pins and machinery.

"Quick! Let's follow him before he gets away!" Fred said. He, Daphne, and Velma started after the monster. But as soon as they crossed the foul line onto the lanes, their feet flew out from beneath them.

Nine-Pin ran over. "Are you kids all right? You can't run on these lanes, you know. Wylie oils them every day to help the balls roll faster."

"But what about that monster?" Velma said. "Don't you want to catch him?"

"That boogeyman got what he came for," Nine-Pin said. "He stole the trophy. What more could he want?"

As the words left Nine-Pin's mouth, the

lights above each lane shut down one by one, until all the lanes were dark. The boogeyman's spooky laugh filled the alley.

"That's it! I'm out of here," one of the bowlers cried.

"Me, too!" said another.

Soon all of the bowlers were making a beeline for the exit.

"Wait! Come back!" Nine-Pin shouted as he ran after the other bowlers. "The tournament's not over!"

"Now it looks like the boogeyman got what he came for," Velma said.

"And so did we, gang," Fred said. "It's time to get to work."

Chapter 6

"If we want to help Nine-Pin salvage the tournament, we have to act fast," Fred said.

"Then we'd better split up," Daphne suggested.

"Good idea, Daphne," Velma said. "Shaggy, Scooby, and I will look around here and on the lanes."

"Fred and I can look for clues around the trophy stand," Daphne said.

"Let's meet back at the control desk in ten minutes," Fred said.

"Come on, you two," Velma said. "Let's get started."

Velma walked over to lane nine. Shaggy and Scooby followed her.

"Keep your eyes out for anything suspicious," Velma said.

"You mean like a bowling boogeyman monster?" Shaggy asked.

"I was talking about clues, Shaggy," Velma said. "I have a hunch there's more to our bowling boogeyman than meets the eye. But the only way we'll know for sure is if we stop talking and start searching for clues. Hey, what's this?"

Velma noticed something on the floor next to the ball return machine. She picked up a small silver bowling pin and examined it closely.

"That's the smallest bowling pin I've ever seen," Shaggy said. "You've heard of a flea circus, Scoob? This little pin looks like it's for the flea bowling league."

Velma studied both sides of the tiny silver bowling pin. "Hmm, this looks like it used to be a pin," she said.

"Uh, excuse me, Velma, but that is a pin," Shaggy said.

"I don't mean a bowling pin, Shaggy," Velma said. "I'm talking about the kind of pin you wear on your clothing. This could be an important clue. Shaggy, you and Scooby keep looking around the lane. I'm going to see if I can get behind it somehow and look for signs of the boogeyman."

Velma carefully walked down lane fourteen to the end. She ducked down beneath the scoring screen and disappeared into the darkness. A moment later, the power for all the lanes came back on.

"I guess Velma found her way back there," Shaggy said. "Do you see any clues, Scooby?"

Scooby looked all around him.

"Ruh-uh," he answered. "Ro rou?"

Shaggy quickly scanned the area.

"Nope," he said. "Since there aren't any more clues, how about a quick game?"

"Rokay," barked Scooby in agreement.

Shaggy picked up a red bowling ball and sent it soaring down the lane. The ball rolled from left to right and rode along the edge of the gutter. Just as it was about to knock down a single pin, the ball fell into the gutter.

"Didja see that, Scooby?" Shaggy asked. "I almost knocked a pin down!"

Scooby picked up a shiny black bowling ball and threw it down lane nine. The ball curved to the right and then to the left and then to the middle. Then it crashed into the center of the pins, sending them flying.

"Rikes!" Scooby barked.

"Nice shot, Scooby," Shaggy said.

"Where's my bowling ball?" a hoarse voice growled.

"It'll be up in a minute, Scoob," Shaggy said. "Just keep your eye on the ball return and be patient."

"Ri ridn't ray ranything," Scooby said.

"Where's my bowling ball?" the voice growled, this time much louder.

"Well, I didn't say anything, either," Shaggy said. "So if I didn't, and if you didn't . . ."

Shaggy and Scooby slowly turned around.

"Rikes!" Scooby cried.

"Zoinks!" Shaggy yelled.

"Boogeyman!" they shouted together.

"GRRRRRRRROOOOOOOAAAARRR!"

Chapter 7

The boogeyman lurched toward Shaggy and Scooby. They stepped backward onto the lane. They tried to run, but the lane was too slippery. Their feet flew out from under them and they fell to the ground, sliding right through the boogeyman's legs.

Shaggy and Scooby jumped up and ran toward a wall of lockers alongside the control desk. They found two open lockers and dived inside, pulling the doors closed behind them.

"Don't make any noise, Scooby," Shaggy whispered. "Or he'll find us for sure."

Shaggy felt something rattle the handle on his locker.

"Zoinks! He found us! So long, Scooby," Shaggy called through the locker. "It's been nice knowing you." He shut his eyes and held onto the door with all his might. Something tugged and tugged at it. Finally, Shaggy couldn't hold on any longer. The door flew open, flooding the small locker with light.

"Please don't hurt me, Mr. Boogeyman," Shaggy said. "I think you're a nice boogeyman. And an excellent bowler."

When nothing happened, Shaggy opened one eye. Fred, Daphne, and Scooby stood there staring at him. Shaggy poked his head out and looked up and down the bowling alley.

"Where's the boogeyman?" asked Shaggy.

"He must have run off right after you saw him," Daphne said. "Because there's no sign of him now."

"What's all the commotion?" Velma asked. She walked up toward the others.

"Shaggy and Scooby say the boogeyman chased them," Fred said.

"Very interesting, but so is what I found behind lane nine," Velma said. She held up a brown bowling ball bag. "It was right next to the track that takes the bowling balls under the lane and onto the ball return."

"Did you find anything else?" asked Daphne.

Velma showed Fred and Daphne the small silver bowling pin they found on lane nine.

"Hey, Scooby, give me a paw, would ya?" asked Shaggy.

Scooby walked over and held out his front paw. Shaggy grabbed it and tried to lift himself out of the locker. Scooby gave a big pull and yanked Shaggy out. He tumbled across the floor and knocked into the trophy pedestal.

"Thanks, pal," Shaggy said. He stood up and dusted off his pants and shirt. He turned around to brush off his shoulders. As he did, Fred, Velma, and Daphne stared at the back of his shirt.

"Like, what is it? Is there a bug on me?" Shaggy asked. "Get it off! Get it off!"

"Hold still, Shaggy," Daphne said. Fred reached out and peeled something off the back of Shaggy's shirt.

"What is it?" Shaggy asked. "A scorpion? A tarantula?"

"It's a piece of tape," Velma said.

"But not just any kind of tape," Fred said. "Look." He put it in his palm and cupped his

hands around it. Daphne and Velma each peered into Fred's hand.

"Is this what I think it is?" asked Daphne.

"You bet," Fred said.

"With all these clues, I'd say it's time to make sure our boogeyman strikes out," Velma said.

"You're right, Velma," Fred said. "Gang, it's time to set a trap. It's clear the boogeyman wanted more than just the trophy. He wanted to ruin Bowlfest and get Nine-Pin to shut down the bowling alley."

"So the only way we're going to get him to come back is to make him think that none of those things is going to happen," Daphne said.

"Like, how are we going to do that?"

"I'm glad you asked, Shaggy," Fred said with a smile.

"Me and my big mouth," Shaggy moaned.

Chapter 8

"**S**haggy, you and I are going to pretend to be the bowling alley mechanics," Fred said.

"Does that mean we get to wear those groovy coveralls?" asked Shaggy.

"As long as Nine-Pin doesn't mind letting us borrow some," Daphne said.

"I don't mind at all," Nine-Pin said, coming up behind them. There were a handful of bowlers standing with him. "I managed to convince a few of the other bowlers to come back."

"That's great, Nine-Pin," Fred said. "We

need everyone we can find to make it look like Bowlfest is continuing. Even you."

"Actually, Nine-Pin, all we really need is one of your bowling shirts," Velma said.

"Who's going to wear one of Nine-Pin's bowling shirts?" asked Shaggy.

Fred, Velma, and Daphne looked at Scooby-Doo and smiled.

"How about it, Scooby?" asked Fred. "How would you like to be a professional bowler?"

"All you have to do is bowl a few frames . . ." Daphne said.

"Rokay." Scooby shrugged.

". . . while you wait for the boogeyman to come back," Velma added.

"Roogeyman? Ro ray!" Scooby barked.

"Come on, Scooby," Fred said. "We're really counting on you."

Scooby sat and folded his paws in front of him.

"Will you do it for a Scooby Snack?" asked Daphne.

Scooby's eyes lit up.

"Ro roy!" Scooby wagged his tail. Daphne took a Scooby Snack from a box and tossed it into the air. Scooby jumped up and gulped it down.

"Let's go get one of your lucky shirts, Nine-Pin," Velma said.

"And some coveralls for the guys," Daphne added.

"Scooby, all you have to do is bowl," Fred said. "Shaggy and I will be standing by, pretending to fix the ball return machine in the next lane. When the boogeyman shows up, you distract him while we capture him with these."

Fred held up some black belts he had taken from the toolbox Wylie left at the control desk.

47

"Are you sure this is going to work?" asked Shaggy.

"Don't worry, Shaggy, everything will be fine," Fred said.

Daphne and Velma returned with the clothing. Fred and Shaggy climbed into the coveralls and zipped them up. Fred grabbed Wylie's toolbox and took it over to the ball return rack on lane nine. Shaggy followed.

Meanwhile, Daphne helped Scooby put on Nine-Pin's shirt.

"Good luck, Scooby," she said.

"Ranks!" he replied.

Velma and Daphne joined the other bowlers and got ready to begin.

"Ladies and gentlemen, welcome back to Bowlfest!" Nine-Pin's voice came over the PA system. "Let the bowling begin!"

With that, the bowlers sprang into action. Balls rumbled down the lanes and crashed into the pins. On lane ten, Scooby picked up a bowling ball and rolled it down the lane and right into the gutter. As Scooby turned around to wait for his ball at the ball return, the other bowlers gasped and stopped bowling. The boogeyman's growl filled the bowling alley.

"Gulp!" Scooby swallowed hard and slowly turned back to face the pins.

"ROOOOAAAAARRRR!"

The boogeyman's glowing eyes zeroed in on Scooby. The monster stood perfectly still at the far end of the lane. It took one, two, then three steps. After the third step, the

boogeyman sent its shiny black ball soaring the wrong way down the lane. It was headed right for Scooby.

"Rikes!" Scooby cried. He jumped out of the way and started running across the other lanes. Glancing over his shoulder, he saw the bowling ball following him!

"Raggy! Relp!" he shouted. No matter where he ran, the bowling ball followed him. The boogeyman howled with laughter as the ball made its way to the front of the lane. Scooby lost his footing and before he knew it, the bowling ball was right behind him. It bumped into his paws, knocking them out from under him.

Scooby recovered by jumping up and grabbing the bowling ball with his paws. His paws ran to keep up with it. Scooby rode the ball up and down the lanes until he found himself heading straight for the boogeyman.

The boogeyman stopped laughing and started running when he saw Scooby coming.

Scooby and the runaway bowling ball chased the boogeyman across the lanes. The monster suddenly lost his footing on the slick floor and belly flopped onto the ground. His hairy body slid along lane nine and crashed into the bowling pins, knocking them all down.

"Rikes!" Scooby barked. He jumped off the bowling ball just before it smashed into the gutter and broke into a million pieces.

Chapter 9

The other bowlers cheered as Fred and Shaggy carefully made their way across the lane to grab the boogeyman. Nine-Pin helped them tie his hands and walk him back to the front of the lanes. They sat the boogeyman at the scoring desk.

"Well, Nine-Pin, would you like to see who the boogeyman really is?" asked Daphne.

"You bet," Nine-Pin answered. He reached over and grabbed the boogeyman's head. With a swift tug, he yanked off the monster's mask.

"Wylie Smithens!" Nine-Pin exclaimed. "I can't believe it. Wylie's the boogeyman?"

"Just as we had suspected," Velma said.

"You did?" asked Nine-Pin. "How did you know?"

"We didn't at first," Daphne said. "But after we found a series of clues, we were able to figure out the boogeyman's true identity."

"What kind of clues did you find?" Nine-Pin asked.

"First we found this," Velma said, showing him the tiny silver bowling pin.

"That looks like a Ten-K Striker Pin," Nine-Pin said.

"It is," Velma said. "And we knew that there were only three people here who had them: Barbara Carbonara, Ham Anndegs, and Wylie."

"I didn't know Wylie had a Ten-K Striker Pin," Nine-Pin said.

"He told us he was, like, one of the first people to ever get one," Shaggy said.

"Isn't that interesting?" Ham Anndegs said from the crowd. He stepped forward and smiled at Nine-Pin. "Even your head mechanic has one, and you still don't."

Nine-Pin gave Ham Anndegs a dirty look, then turned back to the gang.

"What's more, each of those people seemed to have a reason for wanting to cause some kind of trouble tonight," Velma said.

"But then we found the next clue behind lane nine," Fred said. "It was the brown bowling ball bag."

"Something Shaggy and Scooby saw in Wylie's workshop," Daphne said.

"And very much like the one Mr. Anndegs was carrying," Velma said.

"What? Me? I was a suspect?" asked Ham Anndegs. "Preposterous."

"We didn't think so," Fred said. "Espe-

cially when we found out why you retired from the professional bowling circuit."

Ham Anndegs lowered his head and faded back into the crowd.

"If you had told me that back then, I would have guessed Anndegs was behind this," Nine-Pin said.

"We were leaning that way, too," Daphne said. "Especially when we remembered that perfect strike the boogeyman bowled. We figured only a professional bowler could do that."

"That, and know their way around a bowling alley well enough to be able to hide behind the pin-setting machines," Velma added. "But then Shaggy found this. Or should I say, this found Shaggy."

She showed Nine-Pin the tiny piece of tape. She cupped it in her hand like Fred had done before and told Nine-Pin to look inside.

"It's glowing!" he said. "That's glow-in-the-dark tape. Like the monster's eyes."

"And like the tiny stars on Wylie's Robowler bowling ball,"
Fred said. "He used the same tape for the ball and his costume."

"Wylie! Why? I don't understand," Nine-Pin said.

Wylie scowled at Nine-Pin. "I've been the head mechanic at this bowling alley for fifteen years and all you ever cared about was whether your lucky lane was working," Wylie said. "I gave my life to bowling and ended up a mechanic. The Robowler was going to be my ticket to fame and fortune. I planned to melt down the trophy and sell the silver for enough money to build more Robowlers. I was going to infiltrate and take over the professional bowling tour and make millions. Millions! And it was all going along so nicely. Until those kids and their meddling mutt showed up. All that hard work . . . down the gutter!"

"I can't thank you kids enough," Nine-Pin said. "You helped save my bowling alley, even if Bowlfest flopped."

"I wouldn't be too sure about that, Nine-Pin!" Barbara Carbonara called from the front of the bowling alley. She was followed by television camera crews. "One of the bowlers told me what was happening here. I made some calls and here we are! Nine-Pin, this boogeyman thing has made Bowlfest and Drury Lanes the biggest hit in town!"

"And we owe it all to you kids and your dog," Nine-Pin said.

Everyone looked over at Scooby, who was still wearing Nine-Pin's bowling shirt.

"That's my pal," Shaggy said proudly.

"Scooby-Dooby-Doo!" Scooby barked happily.